I0625621

Tales from Across the Realms

A Short Compilation of Short Stories

M. J. Coad

ISBN: 978-1-7635209-2-9 (Paperback)

ISBN: 978-1-7635209-3-6 (E-Book)

Printed by: M. J. Coad

First Printing 2024

By M. J. Coad

Shadows of Ulandir
Heroes of Thered's Field

Short Story Collections
Tales from Across the Realms

<u>Warning</u>

This material contains instances of graphic violence, vulgar language, explicit sexual content, and other such profanities.
It is intended for mature audiences.

Contents

Origin

Every society, every world, has an origin story. Whether it be based upon a cosmological event or some kind of divine intervention. The realms we inhabit are no different. Some have postulated that the reality we know, and occupy, was created in a storm of astral chaos. A thing of chance, nothing more than a fortuitous moment. Most scholars have agreed with this argument, claiming it to be fact. They are, of course, wrong. So very, very wrong.

Wilhem was bored. All around him, his classmates were chattering incessantly as they waited for the professor. About their trivial excursions and adventures during the preceding mid-term break, to far flung realms and distant paradises, each more exotic than the last. About the tavern maids, farmers daughters, and noble princesses that they had taken to bed, all of whom were as least as beautiful as the heroines of legend, oft times more. About everything. About nothing. Wilhem found it tiresome.

They're all full of crap. Spinning tall tales for the chance of gaining some clout with the 'boys.' Pathetic. Truth be told, they're virgins the lot of them, most have probably never even been kissed. Not that there's anything wrong with that. As far as I'm concerned, there's a certain nobility in saving oneself for the right woman. They should just be honest about it.

However, worse than the constant blathering and ceaseless trite nonsense was the heat. Typically, ocean breezes blew across the city of Anátristé, seemingly without end, cooling its residents even at the height of summer. Not so today. Today the air was calm, heavy, hot, and stifling.

Gods, you'd think that as high as we are up this tower, that we'd get a gust of wind or two on occasion, even on a still day. Bugger me it's hot.

Wiping the sweat from his brow with an already soiled handkerchief, Wilhem pulled himself away from the leather cushion of his seat. Stuck from perspiration, his shirt reluctantly peeled off of the aged cowhide, only to cling uncomfortably to his skin. Wilhem sighed.

This is going to be a long day.

A man, whom Wilhem assumed was their professor, strode into the room as though he owned not just the classroom, but the entirety of the university as well. Taller than average, and stouter to boot, he appeared like none of the other professors Wilhem had ever seen before. The way he walked, how he carried himself, reminded Wilhem of a warrior or a soldier, akin to those that served his family on their estate.

Intrigued, Wilhem sat up straighter in his seat, momentarily forgetting the weather as he examined his 'teacher' with a greater level of care. At least part elf, his jawline was sharp and his ears, longer than a human's, swept backwards against the side of his head, ending in fine points. His hair, raven black without a hint of grey, was cut short at the sides, but was long enough on top to flop around as he moved. Beneath his open tweed jacket, which was unusual in and of itself during this heat, a simple black shirt, buttoned in ivory, did nothing to obscure the man's impressive musculature. His pants, also black, clung to his thick calves and well-endowed rear.

I think that most women, and perhaps more than a few men, would be seduced by him as easily as I breath. I'm not interested in him, or any man at all, and yet, even I can see that he's very attractive. It's probably a good thing that there's no girls in this class, they'd probably all be swooning in their seats.

Standing behind his lectern, the professor scanned the room, assessing his students. As his eyes, vivid blue and piercing, met Wilhem's, they lingered for but a moment. A shiver crept up Wilhem's spine and for the first time that day he felt cold.

Gods, those eyes. I have seen them before in killers. Either he is familiar with combat or he is a murderer. Gods, I do hope that it's the former. Either way, I'd best be careful around him.

By the time the professor had finished his examination of the classroom, most of the students had fallen silent, ready for their lesson to begin. However, some holdouts were so engrossed by their conversations, that they were utterly unaware of their professor's presence. The professor didn't bother to call for quiet, instead he just started his lesson, speaking over those who were not yet silent.

'In the beginning there was nothing. Not the nothing that you're used to, empty space just waiting to be filled. Actual nothing. Literal nothing. No space. No matter. Nothing.'

At the professor's first word, those who still spoke immediately ended their conversations and spun to face their teacher. Each, without exception, bore their embarrassment clearly upon their blushing faces.

'I know it might be hard for some of you to wrap your head around this conceptually, especially after your lessons last term, but please try.'

From the front row, Nathaniel, a pompous git dressed in gaudy silks and smelling of cheap powder, whom Wilhem hated more than anyone else he had ever had the displeasure of meeting, blurted out a question, interrupting the professor.

'But sir, how can something be created out of nothing? That makes no sense.'

Of course it doesn't, you moron. Perhaps you should have remained silent and waited for the professor to explain himself. Gods, how I detest you so.

If the professor was annoyed at being heckled, he did nothing to show it. Surprisingly, he just smiled at Nathaniel.

'No. It doesn't, does it? Furthermore, how can something, that is something composed of matter, exist where there is no space, physically if you will, for it to occupy.'

No one answered the obviously rhetorical question. The professor continued, filling the silence with his own voice.

'In short, it can't.'

Leaving his lectern behind, the professor strode casually around the room, all the while continuing his lesson.

'Good morning, everyone and welcome to your second term. As your new professor, it is, first and foremost, my job to build upon the knowledge that you have already accrued, thusly expanding your academic horizons and whatnot. However, before we can move forwards along that adventurous journey, I must challenge what you already know. Or rather, what you think that you know.'

Pausing his speech, but not his movements, the professor wrung his hands together, as if he was considering exactly how to communicate his next thought.

4

'During your last term you were taught that the realms, the space that we all inhabit, exists as a process, or a function, of reality. In other words, it was an accidental creation driven by astral forces and chance. This, as far as I am concerned, and as far as you all should be concerned, is utter nonsense.'

Coming to a halt in the centre of the classroom, the professor turned to face his students.

'Before I explain how the realms really came to be, does anyone have an inkling, no matter how small, as to how I know this?'

Although he was usually never one to be nervous or shy, Wilhem's heart pounded in his chest and his breath shallowed. He knew the answer to question, or at least he thought that he did. Taking a chance, he slowly raised his hand. Instantly, the professor's gaze was drawn to Wilhem.

'Ah, yes, good, we have a taker. So then, what do you think?'

'Well, if the realms were created in an astral event, like an explosion or big bang, then it becomes difficult to explain, logically speaking, how the seven hells, or the divine plane for that matter, are connected to them. We have known for an age that they do not physically occupy space as the mortal realms do, yet traversal between here and there is still possible, so some kind of connection, one that is somehow physical, must exist.'

Wilhem paused, swallowing nervously as the professor's unwavering attention upon him caused his cheeks to grow warm. However, before he could say another word, the professor interjected, his mouth spread wide in a smile.

'Yes! That's it exactly, well done lad.'

Instantly, Wilhem's face cooled, however his heart still raced.

With a wave of the professor's hands, the window shutters snapped shut and the curtains lowered. Instantly, the room was plunged into near absolute darkness.

What in the seven hells is he up to? More importantly, how in blazes did he do that? It seems to me that he is a sorcerer, in addition to everything else.

Some of the students exclaimed loudly, panicked by the sudden change. A scant few left their seats as they attempted to leave the room, but as they were blinded, most tripped, or stumbled, either stubbing a toe or banging a knee. Some even fell over their own feet and ended up on the ground, flailing around like beached fish, confused and impotent. Although he had remained in his chair, Nathenial wailed in protest, the fear evident in his words.

'Sir! What's happening! What have you done!'

Bloody fool. Gods, I swear that you annoy me more and more every day. And the rest, cowards and milksops the lot of them.

Wordlessly, the professor snapped his fingers. A ball of light appeared in his hand and immediately the room calmed. Driven by the professor's will alone, the sphere lifted into the air, expanding as it ascended. Once it reached its zenith, it stopped. Wilhem looked on in awe as at the ball's centre an explosion, one he immediately recognised as a miniature replication of the theorised creation of the realms, spread outwards.

Once the explosion had lost most of its momentum, Wilhem could clearly see an almost perfect model of the realms, each planet, sun, and orbital body represented by a tiny pulsating light. However, he noted that both the seven hells and the divine realm were nowhere to be seen.

Good grief, he just used magic to physically represent my point exactly. That's impressive.

With another snap of his fingers, the light show blinked from existence, the blinds ascended, and the window shutters reopened. In an instant, the room returned to what it had been before, almost as if it had never changed. Sheepishly, those who had panicked during the demonstration, returned to their seats, embarrassment etched deep upon their faces.

The professor paid them no mind, he just continued with his lecture, his attention fixed firmly upon Wilhem, a smile dancing at the corners of his mouth.

'Logically then, if we examine all the evidence, it becomes clear that our realms, all of them, not just the mortal ones, had to have been created by some kind of intelligence. In other words, they exist as a product of, rather than a process of. Now, it is impossible to say with any real accuracy, what form this intelligence took, or if it is a true god, still takes, but that is not important. Whatever 'it' was, or is, can be summed up with the title 'Creator.''

Breaking his stare, the professor resumed pacing around the room.

'Now, I know what you're all thinking, 'a true god?' There are plenty of gods and each of them is true, insofar as they exist. You are of course, correct. However, none of them are powerful enough to create all the realms, let alone half that. And as far as I'm aware, they never have been.'

Pausing his monologue for a moment, the professor glanced sideways at Nathenial, who Wilhem could see, was manically writing down the professor's every word. Although it was only for a moment,

Wilhem smiled as he detected just a hint of disapproval in the professor's eyes for his student.

It seems, chum, that I'm not the only one who finds you annoying. Ha.

'The gods draw their power from two places. The first is obvious, their worshipers. The more followers, the more temples, a god has, the more power they can draw upon to influence the mortal realms. Similarly, the less acolytes, the less shrines, that they have, the less total power they can wield.'

'A god with no followers, and but a single temple, will have long since been cast from the divine realm, yet will still endure. Bound to the mortal realm, they will persist, ageless and unable to die, cursed to resurrect forever more until either their final place of worship is destroyed, and they fade into nothingness, or they gather a new flock of faithful, and they rise re-ascendant.'

Having circled the room, the professor returned to his lectern, standing straight-backed behind it as his attention swept over each of his students.

'The second place is not so well known. In fact, as far as I'm aware, no one alive knows for certain from whence they are derived. I have a theory that they are remnants, echoes if you will, of the Creator and the powers it used to create the realms. To be fully transparent, I have no evidence for this theory, it is, at this time, nothing more than a hunch based upon logic and common sense. Although I believe it to be true, I could, however, be incorrect.'

The professor paused to build the suspense of his forthcoming revelation. Almost giddy with anticipation, Wilhem leaned forward in his seat. Around him, everyone else was deathly silent, even

Nathenial. In that moment, if a pin were to have dropped, the sound it would have made would have been resounding.

'In short, I believe that the origin of the gods powers, that is, the primary source, is the Creator itself.'

Many in the room, gasped in surprise. Some, specifically those who were devout in their religious beliefs, openly scoffed at the professor, charging him with heresy while protecting themselves with a myriad of different hand gestures, each varying according to faith. A few, of which Wilhem was one, remained quiet, keeping their views to themselves.

He's either brave or stupid. I know of more than a few faiths that would have him killed for saying what he did. For saying less than that even. But I respect him for it. A modicum of free thought is far better than any amount of blind obedience. Religious fanatics really do irritate me. Fools.

'However, I will go into detail about that in a future lecture. Now, we return to focal point of this lesson, how the realms came to be. Please remain seated and do not be alarmed, there's no need to be afraid.'

Once more the room went dark, in a much similar manner to previously. Yet this time, there were no cries of alarm, nor panic. Everyone remained firmly planted in their seats.

'I began this lesson with the statemen, 'in the beginning there was nothing,' and it is to this statement where I now return. In the beginning there was nothing, at least in regards to where we are now. Elsewhere there was indeed something.'

As the professor spoke, lights grew from his upturned palms. Whenever he explained a concept, an astrological event, or a change to the universe, the lights shimmered and shifted, playing out the scenes just as the professor described them.

'It is from this 'elsewhere' that the Creator of our realms originated. In an act of supreme power, and no doubt will, the Creator tore through the fabric of his own reality, into the nothingness of nowhere and began to shape the nothing into something. That something, was all that we know today as our reality.'

Out of the darkness, a slit of light opened in the centre of the room. Slowly, the tear widened and a writhing mass of something, a gaseous cloud that Wilhem suspected was the professor's representation of the Creator, oozed out of it. Emanating from the entity, stars, and planets, each a tiny light of yellow, spread out across the room in a perfect representation of the known universe.

Impressive, but I still have my doubts. I wonder if he can prove his claims?

With another snap of his fingers, the professor returned the room to its usual state.

'Now, the astute among you will have noticed that this demonstration is not perfect by any means. Just as with the 'big bang' theory, it does not explicitly explain how the seven hells or the divine realm came to be. Don't worry, that's the subject for a future lesson, not an oversight on my part.'

Pausing, the professor withdrew a small flask, silver and well-polished, from his coat pocket and took a swig. Upon swallowing, his mouth twisted in a grimace, but any discomfort he suffered was taken well in stride, for after he had repocketed the container, he continued as though it hadn't bothered him in the least.

'Of course, as a man of a rational mind and partial to good evidence, I have proof to support my hypothesis. Not in the abstract sense of logical consistencies, but rather, hard proof, physical evidence.'

Some of the students scoffed at the professor's claim, clearly unwilling to believe his assertations, but Wilhem was intrigued. Leaning forward in his seat once more, all the while stroking his chin in thought, he examined the professor's face, searching for any hint of a lie or deception. He only saw confidence.

Whether his claims are true or not, he believes them to be. Very well, I'll entertain his theories, for now at least.

'So then, it is time for me to show you this proof and to do that we must depart our humble classroom. Everyone, please make your way to the observatory, I will be along presently.'

As the student's shuffled out of the room, most eager for a chance to stretch their legs and to converse over what they had just experienced, the professor intercepted Wilhem.

'A word, if you will.'

'Of course, professor.'

Guiding him with an outstretched arm, the professor pulled Wilhem aside, yet said nothing until every other student had left the classroom.

'It is rare for me to have such an astute and unflappable student, tell me what is your name?'

The professor held out his hand. Without hesitation Wilhem took it. At first, he was taken aback by just how firm his teacher's grip was, but then remembered his initial observations of the man, he was more than the typically anaemic academic.

'Thank you, sir. I'm Wilhem, Wilhem von Grumanhieser.'

'Ah, capital, I've heard of your family, of course, but have never had the pleasure of meeting any of your kin, until now that is. Well met Wilhem, my name is J'sa'var and I have a feeling that this is just the beginning of a long and fruitful friendship.'

Exodus

Dragons. Having originated in an unknown realm, far outside our own, their arrival upon Térrtha was witnessed by no one, save for the ancient Dwarves. In none of their discovered texts have they described this event and, by all accounts, no contemporary dwarf-kin remember the tale. Yet, through my own good fortune, I was blessed enough to meet an ancient red dragon. After he had benefited from my services, on several occasions I might add, he told me the tale of why they left their home.

Around Ddraig Goch, an elder dragon of fiery red, the cavern walls shook. A fine mist of dust, dislodged from a long-forgotten alcove far above his head, flittered through the chamber, coming to a rest atop his snout. As he breathed, shallow and calm, the particles worked their way up his nostrils. Responding to the unwelcome intrusion, his sinuses tickled, threatening a sneeze.

Ever aware of just how serious the meeting he was taking part in was, he did his best to avoid any impromptu outburst. Shaking his head, all the while scratching his muzzle with his claws, he tried to work the dirt from his nose before it caused him to sneeze. Too late. Unable to control himself, he inhaled deeply before an explosive sternutation shook his entire body in a wave of shudders. Surprisingly, and without an ounce of intention, a small gout of fire escaped his throat, scorching the cavern floor by his feet black.

Gods, I hope no one noticed me doing that.

Sheepishly, Ddraig peered around the cavern, looking through his parted fingers that hid his abnormally shaded cheeks, which burned

13

hot with embarrassment. While nothing was said, he caught the judgmental stares of several guards and lesser nobles. Evidently, his display demonstrating his inability to control himself had been witnessed by more than just a few.

Here I am, living during the end times of my species, one of the remaining few of my race, and yet, I'm still as awkward as a hatchling not yet endowed with elemental breath. Gods give me strength.

From the far end of the great hall, an expansive space forested with mighty columns in excess of four hundred feet tall and replete with fine carvings along every facet of its walls, a forest green dragon, clad in the silverine armour of the Royal Guard, emerged apace from the grand entranceway. Running with a long, loping stride, he crossed the room in a scant few moments, before skidding to a halt at the foot of Fernyiges's plinth. A bow was the only deference he gave his lord, before he blurted out his message.

'My Lord, the outer defences have been breached.'

Fernyiges, whose pitch-black scales shimmered softly in the torch-light, sighed, heavy and deep, before shifting uneasily upon his haunches.

'It's time. We can wait no longer.'

The room shook again, more violently than before, and a fresh smattering of dirt fell upon the heads of those assembled. From within the crowd, a minor princeling of the blue dragon house, Beithir, exclaimed loudly.

'My Lord, what of Peluda? She has yet to arrive with her clutch.'

Turning his bright yellow eyes to stare at Beithir, Fernyiges bared his teeth, clearly annoyed by Beithir's breach of decorum and the implicit threat to his leadership that Beithir's interjection was.

'If she is not yet here, then she has already been lost. She will be mourned. Later. By others. Now, we have not the time.'

'But my lord! Surely, we cannot abandon her, and the lineage of the whites, so casually. Just a few minutes more, please.'

Enraged, Fernyiges bellowed into the air, spraying a fine mist of acid throughout the cavern. It wasn't enough to harm anyone, diluted as it was, yet Ddraig felt his scales itch at the touch of Fernyiges's breath.

'How dare you! My own house is in tatters, dying with me, and you believe I make the decisions I do on a casual whimsy? No! It is necessary. To wait but a moment longer is to invite utter destruction, the risk is too great. Now, be silent. I have no more to say on the matter.'

Abashed, Beithir knelt in silent surrender, bowing low enough to kiss the ground with his forehead. However, Fernyiges had already turned away from the blue drake, not caring in the slightest for his placations.

'Ddraig, I have one final task for you. Go to the teleportation chamber. Let them know, it's time that the Matriarchs leave.'

For a stunned moment, Ddraig stood frozen, shocked that anyone, let alone the Lord of his kin, would address him directly. A room of jealous eyes, of every hue from white to obsidian, stared at his hide, their incredulous indignation at being passed over in favour of him evident.

Why me? Anyone else would have been a better choice. I'm sure that I'll mess it up somehow, I always seem to. Why did he have to choose me?

Overcoming his nerves, Ddraig gulped in a deep breath of air as his body shook with anxiety, before bowing in respect to Fernyiges.

'I will see it done.'

Or at least I hope that I will.

'Of that I have no doubt. Yet, that is the easy part. Once they've gone you must destroy the circle, before it is seen. The Ophiocordyceps cannot be allowed to follow. Everything will be for naught if they do.'

Ddraig lifted his head, just high enough to meet Fernyiges's gaze.

'I will not fail.'

Gods, I pray that I don't.

'Good. Now, go. We will delay for them as long as we are able, but I fear that the time we gain for you shan't be great. Fly fast, child.'

Ddraig tipped his head in a final sign of respect for his lord. Crouching low, he tensed his body. Coiled tight, just as a spring, he pushed off of the ground, while simultaneously flapping his wings. Gusts of wind, both violent and turbulent, roiled throughout the crowd around him, but it was universally ignored by his kin as nothing more than a minor nuisance. As he shot into the air, a crimson meteor freed from its earthly constraints, his grounded brethren pummelled the floor in a cacophonous salute, bidding him good luck with his task, despite their envy.

Ddraig circled the room but once, weaving throughout the great columns as he flew. With a single glance below him, his chest swelled with pride as he noticed his brethren form ranks, ready to give their lives in the defence of their people's final gambit. Fernyiges, more than a yard taller than any of his fellows, stood at the front, closest to the entrance, ready to be the first to kill and, if it was his fate, the first to die.

Gods, he is such an imposing figure. I find it to be a shame that I could not have spent more time in his service. I could have learned so much. Part of me also wishes that I could stand by his side in the battle to come. Alas, it is not to be. Farewell.

As he neared the top of the cavern, Ddraig passed through an opening within the cave wall. Mirrored by a pair of carved stone dragons, their faces twisted into vicious snarls, their teeth bared in warning, the passage swooped downwards. As it was wide enough for him to traverse while his wings were at their full extension, just barely, it was a relatively easy journey. Yet, it led him to wonder.

I know not how the ancients could have used this tunnel. They would not fit. You'd think that they would have made it wider. Mayber there's another way. Maybe they had to walk, their wings tucked into their sides. Who knows?

Turning this way, and then that, all the while angling lower and lower, the passage opened out into a large room. Although it was not even half the size of the chamber he had just left, Ddraig was still impressed by the three dozen columns, the intricate scrollwork and pictographs that occupied their faces alluding to a level of craftmanship long since forgotten by his kin.

At the far end of the room, a trio of dragons, each smaller than Ddraig, yet clad in armour, stood before a roof-high door, forged from what Ddraig thought to be iron. Covering every inch of its face, carvings of dragons, ancient and otherwise lost to history, depicted the story of his people. From their simple beginnings, to their ascendency over this realm. From the heights of their golden ages, to their eventual decline and almost extinction.

It's strange that it hasn't rusted. Perhaps it's enchanted? No matter. It's no longer important.

Without slowing, Ddraig landed, his impact with the floor kicking up a cloud of dust. Maintaining his momentum, he ran, in a long and bounding stride. Upon seeing his approach, the guards moved to block his passage.

'They're coming! I need to see the Queen. Immediately!'

At hearing Ddraig's warning, each of the guards stood a little straighter and the expressions that they bore upon their faces shifted to reflect the resolute understanding of their impending sacrifice. In unison, they each stepped aside.

'We'll hold them off for as long as we can, but be fast. We three can do little against the horde.'

'Thank you.'

Pushing against the face of the iron door, Ddraig was surprised by the ease of which it moved. With the barest of efforts, the massive entrance way swung open, biding him to enter. He did so, before immediately closing it and barring it with a pair of oak logs that he found standing in a barrel, which seemed to be meant for that purpose.

When it comes to it, this won't hold. I just hope that it gives me a warning when the Ophiocordyceps arrive, perhaps with a few seconds notice I might be able to prepare an ambush. Or at least try too.

Turning away from the door, and entering the chamber proper, Ddraig was met by a circle of seven of his kin, each far larger than himself, standing around an even larger dragon, Tiamat, queen to his people. The very definition of regal, her royal blue scales shimmered with hints of green, in a physical manifestation of the ocean. Clustered in small piles by each of their feet, save for Tiamat's, were a dozen eggs, glittering brilliantly in the flickering torchlight, their shells a mirror image of their mother's scales.

Bowing, as was proper, Ddraig addressed Tiamat directly.

'My Queen, it is time. The Matriarchs must flee.'

From atop her plinth, Tiamat looked down upon Ddraig, her expression blank.

'Peluda is not yet here. We shall wait for her.'

His words positively dripping with desperation, Ddraig forewent decorum and shouted at his monarch.

'My Queen, please, she is not coming. If she were, then she would already be here. You must flee. Now!'

As if to punctuate his desperation, the walls around them shook. In addition, the distant sounds of battle, of guttural screams and roars of both triumph and defeat, wafted into the room. Tiamat narrowed her eyes at Ddraig in judgement, but no retaliatory outburst was forthcoming. Instead, she just shook her head as she sighed.

'Fine. Though it pains me more than you could ever know, we will do as you bid. Now, stand well back, lest you be caught in our spell and leave the path open for our pursuers.'

Ddraig did as Tiamat bid him to, shuffling backwards until his back was hard against the chamber's wall. Then, once Tiamat was satisfied, she nodded to each of the Matriarchs in turn.

'All together now.'

In unison, the Matriarchs bowed their heads and closed their eyes, concentrating on a magic that Ddraig couldn't even begin to understand. A soft glow emanated from the centre of their chests, each a reflection of their own scales, yet pale in the lamplight. Ruby, emerald, sapphire, obsidian, copper, silver, and gold. Each grew to shine as beacons, resplendent beyond description, however none shone as brightly as the font of aquamarine sunlight that surged from Tiamat's heart.

Afeard of being blinded, Ddraig shied away, covering his eyes with his wings. Even doubled over, the membrane did little to obscure the brightness, yet, it was through squinted eyes that he saw, for the first time, the pattern that lay at the matriarchs' feet. Rings of symbols, arcane in their nature, glowed blue, barely visible against the Matriarchs' own light.

The teleportation circle. That is what I must destroy. Erase it before the enemy can discern its meaning. Before they can follow the Matriarchs.

Then, without a sound, the room went dark. Parting his wings, Ddraig looked up, wondering as to what had just occurred. The Matriarchs were gone. Vanished in an instant, their parting devoid of any additional fanfare. However, Tiamat remained. Hunched over and breathing hard, she turned her head to Ddraig, her face an equal merging of triumph and worry.

'Now, it is up to you. Hurry.'

Her lifeforce utterly spent, Ddraig watched on in helpless horror as his Queen's body turned to ash before his eyes. First in small flakes, and then in larger, her scales peeled off of her skin, which in turn parted from her bones. As her flesh landed atop the floor it fell into haphazard heaps, only to disintegrate into absolute nothingness a mere moment later. Eventually, only her skeleton remained, still standing in the exact spot Tiamat had been when Ddraig had entered the chamber.

However, in the end even her bones were lost, departing this realm in a single shower of dust.

Gods, she's dead. My Queen is dead. She sacrificed herself so the Matriarchs could flee. Just like that. By the ancestors, I need to move quickly.

With a haste that was driven by both necessity and worry, Ddraig scrambled over to where the matriarchs had stood when they had disappeared, and to where Tiamat had died. Etched onto the stone floor, as black as coal, was an echo of the arcane pattern he had spotted previously.

How in the seven hells am I going to get rid of this?

At first, he tried wiping it away with his tail. Alas, this did nothing to the symbols, they resisted his attempts so stubbornly that they did not even smudge. Then, he raked the pattern with his claws, trying to carve it from the very stone that it was tattooed upon. In this, he only achieved a modicum of success as some individual runes were rendered indecipherable, but, for the most part, the pattern remained legible.

Not good enough. I don't have time for this. Think Ddraig, why would Fernyiges give you this task over everyone else? Others were of a greater age than I, not to mention a higher station. There must be something I can do that they cannot. Wait. Of course. I'm a fool. Fire. I was the eldest of my house present, save for my Matriarch. The teleportation circles are burned into the stone. My fire can destroy them, or if not, it will at least obscure them.

After inhaling deeply, Ddraig exhaled, mixing his breath with the eternal fire that burned at the base of his throat, unleashing a torrent of flame upon the stone floor. Beneath his fire, the arcane pattern of the teleportation circle gradually disappeared as it was replaced by a sheet of black.

Good. It's working. Albeit slower than what I would have preferred.

From behind him, the door to the chamber shuddered with a heavy thump. Reacting instinctually, Ddraig spun around, the gout of fire that was spewing from between his lips ceasing mid-stream.

They're here. Already. Gods, I've yet to complete my task.

A second impact, heavier than the first, shook the iron door. A myriad of thin cracks spiderwebbed across the logs that held the portal closed, a portent to their immanent destruction. A third impact, as powerful as the second, rang as thunder within the small confines of the room. As heavy as they were, the wood that barred the door was now splintered, teetering upon the precipice of utter destruction. Ddraig could tell, one more strike and they would break.

It has been an age since I have fought in combat, but it appears that on this day, I do so again. Hopefully, I will do better than last time.

Moving to the centre of the room, to give himself room to manoeuvre, Ddraig sat low on his haunches, ready to respond to whoever, or whatever, was about to force its way into the chamber.

With the next blow to the door, the logs that held it closed shattered completely in a shower of tiny splinters. Now free to move, the iron door swung open, denting its frame as it crashed into the wall of the cave. So heavy was the impact, that several large rocks, and more than a few boulders, fell from the ceiling, scattering themselves across the chamber's floor. Strong with fate's blessing, none landed on Ddraig, even if more than a few came close.

Thank the gods, that was close. Too close.

Before another thought could enter his mind, Peluda, but not as he knew her, leapt into the room, her teeth bared into a snarl, her murderous intent clear. Upon first seeing the matriarch, Ddraig paused, not wishing to hurt one of his kin. However, as soon as he noted her eyes, dull-grey, all signs of life departed, and the tendrils of fugus that sprouted erratically from every part of her body, he knew that she was gone, lost to the Ophiocordyceps.

This is not good.

Peluda, or rather what was once her, had no such reservations. Upon seeing Ddraig, she tumbled into the room. Twisting her tail as she rolled, her muscles spasmed and a volley of ice-shard like darts shot through the air at Ddraig.

Still somewhat surprised at being confronted by a matriarch that he had known ever since he had hatched, Ddraig was slow to move. As he leapt to the side, desperately trying to avoid impalement, a trio of the projectiles, far more than what he would have liked, slashed through his wing's membrane. Although the damage was minor, it still hurt and he roared at the pain. Blood vessels punctured, his crimson lifeblood oozed freely, splashing onto the ground as starbursts.

Enraged, not only by his discomfort, but also by the injustice of it all, Ddraig bellowed a gout of flame at the head of what once was Peluda. Afeard that Ddraig's fire would destroy its fungal stalks, thus slaying it, the Ophiocordyceps protected itself by covering its face with Peluda's wings. Leaving not even a mark, the torrent of flame washed harmlessly over the membrane of Peluda's wings.

Argh, gods curse you.

Cutting off the stream of fire, Ddraig bounded over to Peluda's flank. As her sight was obscured by her own wings, she never saw him coming. Growling as he did so, Ddraig swiped his claws against Peluda's side. His claws, as sharp as they were, barely penetrated the ancient dragon's scales, leaving nothing more than a line of shallow furrows and not a hint of blood.

Before Peluda could strike him, Ddraig leapt backwards, barely avoiding the swish of her tail, that would have surely caved in his skull had it connected.

This isn't working. She's too old, too powerful. I'm not sure that I can prevail against her. Gods, what do I do? Damn. I have no choice. I must keep fighting.

With an eerie silence, bereft of any emotion, Peluda chased after Ddraig, slashing her claws, and gnashing her teeth at him as he withdrew. Then, contravening Ddraig's every expectation, Peluda stumbled, tripping upon a rock that her very own actions had placed there.

Now is my only chance.

Seizing the opportunity as it was presented to him, Ddraig pivoted from withdrawal to offence. Leaping across the expanse that separated them, he pinned Paluda to the ground, bending her wings behind her back.

She's stronger than me. I won't be able to hold her for long.

As he sat atop her, Peluda's claws slashed deep into his underbelly, rending chunks of flesh from his bones with every swipe. The agony he felt was the worst he had ever endured, yet he held on, accepting the pain as a necessary sacrifice.

Now, I can see how to win. Victory will be mine.

Holding Peluda's jaws open with his foreclaws, Ddraig drew into his body a lung full of fresh air. Then he exhaled. A torrent of liquid fire, as hot as molten magma, poured from his mouth into Peluda's. He was a red dragon and fire was his element, heat was a meaningless of a concept to him as time was to the Creator. She was not. She was a white, her element ice. Fire was her bane.

As her insides melted, the physical remains of Peluda writhed in a macabre dance born from the amalgamation of anguish and desperation. With the sudden rise of her core temperature, the mycelial network, the roots of the Ophiocordyceps that granted them control over their victims, spontaneously combusted. In but a moment, the Ophiocordyceps's entire root system flared as black powder igniting. This served to facilitate a chain reaction within the fungus, and thusly, the body of the Ophiocordyceps, the external fungal stalks, similarly caught fire.

The body of Peluda gave a final spasm as the Ophiocordyceps crumbled to dust, and was then still, returned to death once more. Breathing heavy, Ddraig released Peluda's corpse, gently lowering her to ground, his care for his old friend still evident in his mournful stare.

Victory, but I find it hollow. It was not worth the cost. Now, revered one, be at peace forever more.

As he arched his neck, so his forehead touched Peluda's brow in a final act of farewell, Ddraig's legs wobbled. It was in that moment, barely able to stand, his muscles on the verge of capitulation as his blood poured from his many wounds, Ddraig knew that he was going to die. There was no chance of escape, no hope for life. There was nothing he could do to avoid it. A calm, born from acceptance, washed over him. His heartbeat slowed and his rapid breathing eased.

25

If I am to die, then my final act will be what guarantees my people's future.

Closing his eyes, he focused his attention towards the centre of his being. There, at his heart, pulsed an orb of brilliant red, the physical manifestation of elemental fire. Pouring his will into the ball, Ddraig coaxed energy from it, transferring its power into himself. At first it came as a trickle, slow but steady. His scales started to tingle as his senses superseded their normal limits. The most subtle of smells, normally undetectable to everyone, and the most distant of sounds, far beyond the realms of regular hearing, all become as clear as crystal to him. The pain he felt grew to that of an immeasurable burden, yet the eldritch powers growing within him offered a euphoric balm that rendered his torment moot.

I can hear them, the Ophiocordyceps. They're coming. All my kin are dead. I am the last.

Then the power came as a flood, surging into every one of his atoms. Filling them so they sung in a glorious chorus. He had never felt so alive, so powerful, as what he did in that moment. However, he still craved more. He still needed more.

They're close. So very close. It must be now. I pray that it will be enough.

As the hordes of Ophiocordyceps skittered over Peluda's lifeless husk, Ddraig released all of the energy he held. In less time than it took for his heart to beat, his body vanished as it went supernova. A wave of power, vast beyond all mortal comprehension, swept across the chamber, vaporising everything in its path. No Ophiocordyceps, no dragon, no flesh, no metal, no rock. Nothing could stand against its fury.

From a distance, the mountain of Hursag seemed to disappear. One moment it was there, as tall, and as imposing as ever, the next it was simply gone.

Midnight Love

Most stories are lost to the infinite abyss of time and forgotten. But some are so profound that they are remembered. This is one such tale. It is not a complete account by any means, for those whom it pertains to rarely suffer the questions of others. It is however, all that we know of the Forest King's first love and her ascension from mortal to the first Queen of the Fae, ageless progenitor of the Woodland Elves.

Enraptured by the serene beauty of the tri-moons of Térrtha, Ercel stared out of the kitchen's window wistfully as their heavenly procession crawled across the star-plastered sky. Within her chest she felt the itch of longing bloom, for what, or whom, she knew not. Yet, in that moment, it was clear to her, as distinct as the moons themselves, that something was missing from her life. Someone was missing from her life.

Not for the first time that day, she wondered what it would be like to live another life. To be somewhere else, wearing someone else's skin. To be a princess or a queen, an adventurer, or a sailor. To live in a grand palace or a well-kept townhouse. To catch the eye of a handsome prince and claim his heart for her very own. To be more than a farmer's daughter, shackled by the constant stream of chores and the inevitable loveless marriage that her father had planned for her. In short, she sought agency, to live as she saw fit and to love whomever she deigned to love.

Why shouldn't I get to choose my fate? Why shouldn't I be whomever I want to be?

'Ercel! Cease your stargazing this instant!'

Startled from her daydreaming, Ercel jumped at her grandmother's words, almost dropping the plate that she was drying in the process. With great care, she sat the dish in the rack, lest it slip from her grasp and shatter. Only then, her face scrunched up in confusion, did she turn to face her grandmother.

'But why grandma? Where's the harm in looking at the moons? I mean, they're just, well, um, rocks really.'

Ercel's grandmother sighed in defeat before abandoning the pot that she was scrubbing.

'There be a power in the tri-moons, a power I can't say tha' I rightly understand, but a power nonetheless. Come on lass, leave tha' be and follow me.'

Ever eager to get out of doing chores, Ercel threw her dishcloth down and followed her grandmother with a barley suppressed glee. As their house, that being the farmhouse that Ercel, her grandmother, and her father occupied, was small and simple, their journey was short. After rounding but a single corner, the pair entered the living room.

Ercel's grandmother pointed to the armchair in the corner and uttered just one word.

'Sit.'

Despite its age, and the myriad of unidentifiable stains that covered its surface, it was one of the most prized possessions of their household. A family heirloom which had been constructed before her grandmother had been born, it was only ever sat in by the eldest family member. Up until this point in time, Ercel had only ever known her grandmother to use it.

Grandma never lets anyone sit in her chair, let alone me. I wonder why she's allowing me too now? Oh well, I shan't complain.

Ercel did as her grandmother bid and lowered herself onto the armchair. Immediately, she sunk into its plush cushions, almost disappearing within their embrace. Just as she had expected, it was immensely comfortable, cushy beyond all measures of reason.

Wow, this is amazing. I feel as though I could fall asleep in just a moment of rest. I hope grandma lets me use it more often.

'Now, what I'm about to tell you is a cautionary tale, one tha' you should heed. My granny told it to me when I was just a lass, nary a day older than what you are now, and before tha' her granny told it to her. One day, gods willing, you'll also tell it to your granddaughters.'

Bending over, Ercel's grandmother reached into her knitting bag, that never left her chair's side. After several moments of rummaging around, and more than a few muttered curses, she pulled out a small brown book. Clearly marked by age, its cover was scratched in several places and its binding was barely holding it together. Compelled by curiosity, Ercel examined the book's cover intently, trying as hard as she could to make out its title. However, either it had never had a title or it had long since faded, for she could make out nothing.

'Is it a true story?'

'Hm, I'm not sure, but I don't think tha' matters one bit. Now quiet, I'll brook no interruptions while I'm telling this tale.'

Without further ado, Ercel's grandmother opened the strange little book and began to read.

*   *   *

Even though she had long since retired for the evening, Caitlin was unable to sleep. Agitated, she tossed and turned in her bed, hoping to find the exact position she needed to succumb to slumbers embrace. Useless. No matter how she tried, sleep would just not come.

Taking a deep breath, she tried to force the myriad of thoughts that roiled relentlessly around her brain out of her mind. Much to her annoyance, they refused to leave her be.

Gods, why do I have to marry someone I barely know? Is true love, the kind that the speak of in the fairytales, too much to ask for? And why now? Tomorrow's only my seventeenth name day, why can't father give me more time to find someone I actually want to be with? Gods, why me? It's so unfair.

Frustrated beyond measure, Caitlin gave up her attempts at sleep and threw her bedsheet aside in a huff.

A walk, that's what I need. To settle my thoughts, to calm down. I'll never get to sleep like this.

Careful to be as quiet as she could, lest she wake her parents, Caitlin tiptoed out of her bed and fetched yesterday's dress from the nightstand. With a haste bordering on manic, she pulled it down over her shift, smoothing out its wrinkles the best that she could. It was a simple thing, coloured in a single shade of light-green and knitted from a coarse wool, but from what she owned, it was by far her favourite.

That'll do. It's still warm enough to not need anything else.

With her heart pounding in her chest, as both the fear and the anxiety of being caught flooded her bloodstream with adrenaline, Caitlin eased the front door of her farmhouse open. As it squeaked in protest, she swallowed nervously, worried that it had betrayed her.

Nothing. No shouts of alarm, no slapping of her parents' feet as they hurried to investigate a strange sound in the night. Nothing.

Relieved, Caitlin breathed out in a heavy sigh and stepped outside. Before she could let her own rational mind convince her that her actions were foolish and dissuade her from pursuing her desires, she closed the door behind her and took three rapid steps away from her house.

There it's done. I'm out. There's no point in turning back now. I may as well do what I intended.

With a cheeky grin, identical to the one all troublemakers wear while in the midst of doing what they should not be, Caitlin skipped down the dirt track that bordered her family's home. Free from the stifling confines of her bedroom, and buoyed by the night air's warm caress, she no longer feared discovery, in fact she revelled in her liberty. Unable to contain her mirth, she laughed, a melody as sweet as windchimes.

Abruptly, the path she followed ended in a wall of trees. The woods before her gave her pause. During the daytime she would have entered the forest without a second thought, in-between chores she often wandered amongst the pines and spruce. But, to enter the woods at night? That was an altogether different proposition, one that involved all manner of nocturnal creatures, predators both large and small. There was a risk, albeit small, that if she ventured into the forest, she would never return.

Bah, I'll be fine. I'm sure that absolutely nothing can go wrong. I mean, I can't think of a single thing that could.

With a shrug of her shoulders, she continued onwards, skipping into the woods with only a modicum of care. Many a twig snapped under her feet, and many a shrub rustled, as she passed, but Caitlin thought nothing of it, never once considering to whom, or to what, she was announcing her presence to.

It was dark within those woods, but not entirely so. As this was the night of a tri-moon, soft rays of celestial light, white, orange, and yellow, were able to penetrate the forest's canopy, providing her with a means to guide her journey. She knew just where she was going, for she had been there many times before.

Emerging from a dense thicket of tamarack, Caitlin found herself within a clearing, her desired destination. At the centre of the glade, she sat atop a lichen covered log and stared up at the night sky. A sea of golden pinpricks shimmered upon a blanket of obsidian. Within that tapestry of colour, the tri-moons of Térrtha floated lazily by, totally irreverent to the tribulations of those below.

It must be past midnight by now. That means I'm seventeen. My coming-of-age day. The day of my marriage. Gods, I wish it wasn't so. I mean, Hamish is a good man, and not at all ugly, if perhaps not handsome, but I don't love him. Perhaps I could one day, but I don't want to find out. I just want something more. Something better. Something different.

A shooting star flew past, a fiery trail of burning debris following in its wake. To where it was going and to whence it came, she knew not, but Caitlin closed her eyes and muttered a wish under her breath.

Gods please, I bid of thee, let me know true love.

Slowly, she opened her eyes, sighing at her unfulfilled fancy. Gazing upwards, she returned her attentions to the unfathomable beauties of the night sky. She was utterly enthralled by what she witnessed, the mysterious nature of the heavens only extenuating their already palpable charm. Curious by nature, she couldn't help but to wonder what glorious secrets lay beyond the known realms and wistfully dreamt of being the one to discover them.

If only I could travel the stars.

Out of nowhere a carpet goosepimples sprung up on her bare skin. Not for cold, for it was uncharacteristically warm for this time of year, and in any case, she usually revelled in chilly climes, but for a gentle breeze. It tickled her flesh in the most stimulating of ways, exciting her senses and enlightening her as to what it meant to be alive. Taken in its grasp, her raven hair fluttered freely around her trim, yet curvaceous, figure whipping this way and then that. She did nothing to tame it, feeling that to break its wild spirit would be tantamount to a crime.

A sudden gust of wind, far stronger than any of the others, rustled through the tree branches. Loosed from their bonds, autumn kissed leaves of golden amber fell slowly through the air above Caitlin's head. Spinning and twisting, they floated towards the ground, but before they could make landfall they were caught by the breeze. Ensnared as they were, the breeze spun them around Caitlin, just as the dust in a snow globe drifts around the snowman. Delighted, she watched their elegant dance and her mouth curled upwards in unbridled joy.

Caitlin's mirth was short lived as the breeze soon grew in force. Rising in power, from a wind most gentile to a wild maelstrom. It did no harm to Caitlin, but the leaves floating around her were captured within the tempest. Faster and faster, they spun, A wall of blurring green, absolute and impenetrable, Caitlin could see nothing beyond their whirling forms.

She knew not why, but for some indecipherable reason she felt compelled to reach out her hand and touch the vortex. A surge of pain seared through her as a single leaf sliced the tip of her finger. With a startled yelp, Caitlin withdrew her hand and held it to her chest. Eyes furrowed, she examined the wound. A thin red line blemished her perfect porcelain complexion. Her blood welled and a single crimson drop fell to the forest floor. She sucked her finger, preventing more blood from spilling. However, the proverbial damage had been done, for one drop of blood was all it took to enact the ancient and slumbering magics of the wild.

In an instant, the leaves stopped spinning, all vestiges of wind gone. They hung in midair frozen. Caitlin's curiosity gave way to concern.

What strange magic is this? Was it me, did I do this? Oh gods, what have I done?

All around her, Caitlin felt the air crackle with an electrical force as sparks of eldritch blue forked between the hanging leaves. All the oxygen seemed to be forced from her lungs and she was forced to sit, gasping for relief as she struggled to breath.

Oh gods, I'm going to die. Please gods, I don't want to. Not yet.

On the verge of unconsciousness, Caitlin both heard and felt an explosion. Resounding throughout the glade, a wall of force sent her tumbling across the ground. When she came to a rest, sprawled onto her back and still unable to breathe, she looked up at the floating leaves, untouched by the explosion. Spontaneously, they accelerated to supersonic speeds and in an instant, they disappeared, flying off into the woods.

What in the seven hells is happening?

Just as the leaves departed, her breath returned. Sitting up, hunched over at the waist, she breathed hard, thankful for the blissful relief that the fresh air provided.

Gods, that was close. I thought I was about to die. I almost did.

The snap of a twig startled Caitlin, as far as she knew she was alone. Without a second of thought, she turned towards the sound, before gasping in surprise.

Before her stood a strange and wonderful man. He was so very tall, easily the tallest man Caitlin had ever seen. His eyes shone as a firefly would, yellow tinged with the barest hint of green. Within those eyes, Caitlin could see a deep and unsettling ferocity simmering just beneath the surface. This was not a man whom one should ever cross, lest that fire surge to an inferno. However, within them, Caitlin also saw a tenderness that belied any preconceptions of unwarranted malice.

Wispy hair of mottled green and brown, dangled loosely past his shoulders. His muscles rippled under his taught skin, bulging biceps and chiselled abs. Their magnificence was extenuated by the man's lithe motion as he slowly stalked towards Caitlin. Unbidden, Caitlin felt the stir of attraction from the pit of her stomach.

As she examined the man, enraptured by his exquisite form, Caitlin's eyes drifted lower. She felt the betraying burn of a blush spread over her checks as she took in the glory of the man's exposed manhood. She was not completely naive, she was a farm girl and knew well the basic principles of reproduction, she had in fact seen many a beast in rut. However, she had never witnessed the male anatomy of a human, or in this case a humanoid, so explicitly in the flesh before. A

Atop a patch of discarded leaves, the pair lay entwined, their sweat soaked bodies heaving as they puffed from exertion. Caitlin turned to the man, the widest of smiles fixed firmly across her face. The man beamed in return, his grin matching her for both width and sincerity. Spontaneously, Caitlin grabbed the man's hand and forced him to his feet. Holding him close, Caitlin started to sway, the man swaying with her.

The moons as their spotlights, the pair danced, naked and free, unabashedly in love. For hours and hours their sultry dance continued. Every so often, they would stop to make love, but as soon as they had each achieved climax, their dance would resume. This cycle of frolicking and fornication continued until, in the wee hours of the morning, at last they were both utterly spent.

It was then that the man led a still-naked Caitlin through the forest to the base of the Great Pine. Waving his hands, all the while chanting arcane phrases she did not understand, the bark of the tree morphed and shifted. Slowly, it parted to reveal a shimmering wall of pulsating green energy.

Is that a portal? To where does it go, I wonder?

Trepidation weighed heavily upon Caitlin's heart and for a moment she hesitated. She loved the man and she would do anything for him, that much she knew, but to abandon her family without a single word of farewell? That was a bitter potion to swallow, let alone force upon another. Sensing her reluctance, the man took Caitlin's hand and kissed it. With a single, loving smile, all her worries and fears fled, gone in little more than a heartbeat.

Everyone will be fine without me. In fact, if they knew what had happened, what I've found, they'd all be happy for me.

Reassured once more that the path she followed was the correct one, Caitlin let the man, whom still held her hand in his, lead her into the portal. Once they were both through, it closed. The tree's bark reforming back to its original state, leaving not a trace of Caitlin, nor the man.

*   *   *

Ercel's grandmother closed the book shut with a curt snap. Instantly, the visions of Caitlin and the forest stranger dissipated from the forefront of Ercel's mind. Once more in the real word, Ercel sat mute, astounded that her grandmother would so openly recount such an erotic and scandalous tale.

I wonder why grandma told me a story that was so, well, um, visceral and, um, invigorating. Not that I'm complaining, I rather enjoyed it. Um, perhaps a bit too much in fact.

'There, it's done. Let tha' be a lesson to you. Strange things happen under the light of a tri-moon, it'd be for the best to just stay inside and not tempt fate. And tha' means no staring at the moons either! Magic has a strange way of affecting young lasses' brains.'

If there was a moral to that story, I'm not sure that I understood it. For the most part it sounded like everyone involved had the best of times. Multiple best of times in fact.

As she remembered, vividly so, the intimate moments within her grandmother's tale, Ercel's face flushed scarlet. Deeply embarrassed, she wanted nothing more in that moment than to leave, to return to her chores or, and it pained her to admit it, to turn in for the evening. Anything that did not involve Caitlin, the man of the forest, or her own arousal, would have suited her fine. Yet, ever curious, a question that lingered in her mind demanded an answer.

'Grandma, who was the man? From the story I mean. Do you know?'

'Hm, I don't know dear. My mother, a woman far more educated than me, thought tha' it could be the King of the Forest, Lord of the Fae, and the father of the wood elves. But I'm not sure if tha' could be true. For as long as our family has told tha' story, and we've been tellin' it for an age, the King of the Forest is much older by far.'

'Could he have just been an ordinary elf?'

Her grandmother just shrugged.

'Maybe. Tha's more likely than him being the King of the Forest, but, bah, who am I to say? Now, tha's enough questions for one evening, off to bed with you.'

Glad to be free of such an awkward situation, Ercel skipped to her room, stripped to her undergarments, and dove under her bedsheets, eager to be asleep after a long day of chores.

Later that night, long after she had retired, Ercel awoke, drenched in sweat. The remnants of a dream, so vivid that it burned as clear as daylight in her mind, raced around her brain. In her vision, if that was what it really was, she had been Caitlin, the girl from her grandmother's tale, and it had been her that had lain with the stranger.

A slew of thoughts and questions raced around her mind. Did the dream hold a deeper meaning, one lost beyond rational comprehension? Did it speak to her own carnal desires? If it would have been her to encounter the woodland man, would she have given herself away as easily as Caitlin had? Would she have fallen in love with the stranger? Ercel knew none of the answers to these questions, yet a part of her wished that she had the opportunity to discover them.

A walk. That's what I need. Just to clear my head. I shan't be able to sleep otherwise.

Careful to be as quiet as she could, lest she wake either her father or her grandmother, Ercel threw her bedsheets aside and crept from her bed. Fetching yesterday's dress, a simple woollen garment of a light-green hue, from the top of her dresser, she pulled it down over her shift. Then, with an equal amount of care, she tiptoed out of the house and down the dirt track that bordered her home. For whatever reason, the woods called out to her and she had decided that she would respond.

Thaddeus the Eternal

The dwarves of these lands were not always as they are now. Many eons ago, they ruled supreme over Ulandir, their empire stretched far and wide. But, like any that dare to fly to close to the sun, they were burned. Their ruler, whose name has long been lost to history, tempted fate by offending one even more powerful than he. Decades of war ensued and the Empire of the Dwarves crumbled. If not for the selfless sacrifice of one brave dwarf and his courageous companions the dwarves would have likely been rendered extinct. It is for his sacrifice that he is remembered, and so will it always be, as long as there is a single dwarf that still draws breath. In this way he achieved a kind of immortality that very few do. This is all that we know of his tale, undoubtedly there is more to the story, but as with all things, time is the universe's great eraser.

The wind stung Thaddeus's face as his rockclimber lumbered across the rolling plains. His entire body ached, as he had been riding non-stop for several days, and his current mount had been driven to the verge of death. However, stopping was not an option. The news he carried was too important, the Council had to be notified of the approaching peril. Thankfully, his destination was close. If he maintained his current pace, he would reach it by midafternoon.

Just as the sun was reaching its zenith, Thaddeus crested a boulder-strewn knoll and the walls of Solidum Liquatur came into view. Exhaling in a sigh of relief, Thaddeus spurred his mount onwards, eking out the last vestiges of its energy.

Upon seeing his approach, the city guards, hidden from his sight, broke open the great oak gates. As they swung inwards, welcoming him home, Thaddeus patted the neck of his mount, encouraging it for one final time. Not slowing as he crossed the city's threshold, his rockclimber's cloven hoofs clattering loudly on the stone paved street, he raised his voice, so he could be heard over the din, and shouted as he rode.

'Summon the Council! Let me be heard, summon the Council! To any, and all, summon the Council at once!'

Reaching the end of the main thoroughfare, Thaddeus leapt from his rockclimber. Utterly spent, the beast keeled over into a heap. A final exhale of breath was all it could manage before it expired. Grateful for its sacrifice, Thaddeus tipped his head in salute.

I'm sorry my friend. I wish it wasn't so, but my need, and the need of my people, was great.

Too tired to travel at any great speed, Thaddeus set out from there at a brisk walk. Dwarves, of every age and occupation, joined him on the street, each having heard his cry for the Council to assemble. As one roiling mass, they wound their way through the city, their destination the same. As they travelled, their numbers grew and all around him the throng sung with rumours. Most were fanciful, claiming that the war had been one, yet some brushed so close to the truth that Thaddeus worried that the city would fall under the spell of a full-blown panic before a plan could be devised, let alone implemented.

Remain clam for just for a moment longer, that's all I ask.

Pushing his way   into the Council Chambers, through the gathering crowd, Thaddeus sat in the first unoccupied chair that he

46

found and waited. One by one, the Councillors entered the hall and took their respective seats; all save for a lone dwarf who milled about near one of his fellows. Even after affording the Councillor nothing but a cursory glance, Thaddeus couldn't help but to see the hate for him, crystal clear in his eyes, as the disgruntled Councillor stared unwaveringly in his direction.

He knows that it was me that called the meeting. How, I do not know, but that must be it. But that alone is no reason for such hatred. I wonder what has him in such a sour mood? Bloody prick.

The last to arrive was the Chief Councillor himself. As he strode across the Chamber's floor, his long robes dragging across the polished marble, he roared a question.

'What is the meaning of this? Who has summoned us and why?'

Thaddeus stood and bowed in deference to the elderly statesman.

'My apologies to the council, and to my Lord specifically, it was I who called this meeting.'

Rage, pure and simple, burned across the face of every councillor. Their cheeks red, breathing shallow, each were upon the precipice of exploding. The gall of a humble legionary, of no standing whatsoever, to call them, every one crucially important to the city, to assemblage. It was unheard of. It was scandalous. Yet somehow, the Chief Councillor remained calm.

'Why?'

Thaddeus bowed even lower.

'Again, I apologise for my intrusion upon the city my Lord, but I am afraid that the news I carry is most dire and I could not wait for even a moment to share it. I have returned from the Northern front to report that our forces have been defeated. All who are not dead have been routed, scattered across the countryside. The enemy will no doubt already be on their way here and there's no one left to stop them.'

The chamber erupted in a chorus of angry cries and exclamations. Council members stamped their feet upon the floor and banged their hands against the table before them. They were clearly not pleased. Raising his hand for silence, the Chief Councillor calmed his fellows. Turning to Thaddeus, he sought clarification.

'I don't believe this nonsense! How in the seven hells were our armies defeated by some human barbarians.'

Rising from his bow, Thaddeus remembered the blood and the guts of battle. Of dwarves voiding their bladders and bowels as they died, screaming for their mothers, crying out for mercy, and finding none. He sighed.

'It's true my Lord, they are savages, in every sense of the word, but they had us outnumbered. By at least ten to one. Ours were by far the superior troops, but they overwhelmed us. Given the unfavourable field of battle and other, unforeseeable, circumstances, there was no way that we could have achieved victory. I'm sorry, my Lord.'

Like a dwarf who had just tasted merlot for the first time, the Chief Councillor took a while to consider what Thaddeus had just told him. He rolled it around in his mind, tasting it, trying to decide if the flavour suited him. From his scowl, it was clear that it did not, yet when he responded, he did so in a slow and measured tone.

'By the gods, what shall be done now? The King will not sue for peace. He would rather his people die than see them capitulate. And if our armies are, as you say, destroyed, then that is what will surely come of us when the barbarian horde launches their inevitable offensive against us.'

The Council Chambers were deathly silent as everyone present hung on the Chief Councillor's every word. As the dwarf paused, to gather his thoughts, or to perhaps internally practice the delivery of a hard truth, Thaddeus knew not, the air within the Chambers hung heavy with apprehension. The Chief Councillor sighed, breaking the deathly silence.

'I must admit, I am no military man. I am well past the years of my youth, and even in a leadership role I would struggle, I've not the mind for it you see. So, as you are a soldier and as such more qualified, I ask of you, what do you recommend we do, legionary?'

Gods, he's asking me what to do. I'm not qualified for this. What do I say. I need a plan.

A thin sheen of sweat formed upon Thaddeous's brow. His heart raced in his chest and his palms grew clammy. He was only a legionary, the lowest of ranks, and a Chief Councillor was asking him what an entire city should do. The responsibility, the pressure, it was so much, too much for him to bear. Yet tolerate it he must, there was no choice. He needed to think of a plan, and fast.

'I am humbled that a noble dwarf such as yourself would ask the opinion of one so simple as myself, thank you. As far as I see it, there is only one course of action open to us. We must flee.'

For the second time in just as many minutes, the chamber exploded in a cacophony of angry and disapproving shouts. Thaddeus raised his hand apologetically for silence, but it was only when the Chief Councillor did the same, that the din in the chamber ceased. Thaddeus nodded his thanks to the Chief. In response, the elder gestured for Thaddeus to continue.

'Thank you again my Lord. I know just how much our people detest giving in to those that would take from us. If it were only my life that was in the balance, I would have died before dishonouring our people. However, in this instance it is not just my own life, but everybody's. We have no choice. Either we give what is ours willingly or it will be forcibly rent from our cold, dead hands. If we run, at the very least, we will still have our lives and the lives of our loved ones. Our people, nay our legacy, will persist. We will endure.'

Thaddeus paused and examined the faces of those around him, gauging their reactions to what he had just said. It was clear that they were angry, their faces scowled at him, their eyes burning with disdain. Knowing full well that they still needed convincing, Thaddeus forged ahead and began to outline his plan.

'I seek to table a motion of action. Our women, children, elders, and any others not able to wield a blade will leave as soon as able, preferably on the morrow, for the capital. All of those able to fight will make for the Septentrionalem Pass. It is narrow and the humans will have to travel through it if they wish to enter our lands proper, a perfect chokepoint. There we will make a stand, both to give the rest of our people time to flee and to exact a heavy as possible toll on their forces. They will rue the day that they dared to stand against us!'

As Thaddeus finished his speech, the Council Chambers were deathly quiet. The Chief Councillor sat stroking his beard in contemplation, staring intently at Thaddeus, as if examining his very soul. After a moment he broke the silence with a whisper.

'Do you truly believe that this is our best chance?'

Thaddeus responded in a certain tone; his conviction evident.

'No, my Lord. I believe it to be our only chance.'

'Hm, I see but a single flaw in your plan. You would leave our people defenceless upon our journey. No doubt the humans are the greatest threat, but the roads south have grown perilous in recent months.'

Damn it, I should have seen that. Have a care Thaddeus, one more mistake could ruin everything.

Thaddeus dipped his head in respect to the elderly statesman.

'My apologies, Councillor, you are, of course, correct. I would offer but a single amendment to my plan. I will split our forces, leaving behind more than enough to guard our people, while taking the rest north to confront the humans.'

'Hm, that is acceptable. Let us make it so. Legionary! Muster our forces and lead them to the pass. You will assume command for this mission. I will provide you with my seal as proof of your mandate. May the gods guide your soul through to the great beyond.'

Placing a closed fist atop his heart, Thaddeus bowed.

'Thank you, my Lord. I will do our people proud, by our ancestors I swear it.'

'Of that, my son, I have no doubt. On behalf of our people, I thank you.'

Straitening his back, Thaddeus slammed his fist against his breastplate. Although the Chief Councillor was finished with him, and he had much to do, he dared not leave the hall in the middle of the assembly, so he retook his seat.

Well, I'm not sure that could have gone any better. He both listened to me and agreed with my plan, for the most part, as hastily thought up as it was. Hm, a heroic last stand. It's not the way I would have chosen to go out, but it's better than what most get.

Lost in thought as he was, a gentle tapping on his shoulder caused him to jump. Turning to see who it was, and what it was that they wanted, Thaddeus was surprised to be met by the piercing gaze of an abnormally attractive woman.

Close to his own age, slender, yet curvaceous in all the right ways, she held in her hand the Chief Councillor's writ. With a nod of thanks, he took the roll of parchment.

As the woman walked away, he couldn't help but to admire the way her hips swayed and how tightly her silk dress clung to her perfect figure. Almost as though she knew, the woman looked behind her, catching Thaddeus in his lechery. However, she didn't seem to mind. A playful smile and a casual wink were his reward.

An invitation for later perhaps? Bah, there's no doubt that she's stunning, but as far as I'm concerned, her beauty doesn't come close to matching Karissa's.

He had stopped listening to proceedings some time ago, but a loud shout from the Chief Councillor drew his attention back to what was being said.

'Councillors! See to your clans, gather only the barest necessities for a long journey. Tomorrow, we march!'

The Council Chambers exploded with frantic movement as everyone present, from lowly peasants to high caste nobles, sprung forth, eager to do as bidden. As he was in as much of a hurry as everyone around him, Thaddeus let himself be pulled along by the crowd, not that he had any choice. At the first opportune moment, he broke free of the throng and, with all the haste he could muster, jogged directly to the city's military outpost. He had other business to attend to, but that had to wait.

Standing as a towering beacon of dwarven resilience, the outpost was girted by a tall stone wall of black basalt. A single gate of ancient oak, a smaller cousin to the city's own, marked its only entrance. Currently it was open, as there was no reason for it to be shut.

Hopefully this won't take long. I need a nap. Then I need to find Karissa, we need to have a conversation.

Strong with purpose, Thaddeus strode through the gate, looking for anyone who could assist him. In the centre of the yard, he saw a Centurion instructing some of the newer legionaries as to the finer points of swordplay. Walking up to the Centurion, Thaddeus slapped his fist to his chest in salute and held up the Chief's writ.

'Centurion, I have orders from the Chief, muster the legion for inspection.'

Although Thaddeus was a lower rank than him, the Centurion noted the Chief's writ and slapped his chest with his fist.

'Sir, it will be done at once.'

Walking to the head of the parade grounds, Thaddeus waited for the legion to assemble. He did not have to wait for long. Soon after the Centurion had run off, a horn blared three times from the central keep's roof. Immediately, dwarves began pouring from the barracks and the mess alike. Each wore their plate armour, polished to a bright shine, proudly on their chests. In their hands they carried their scutum's and upon their belts swung a bevy of throwing axes, alongside their signature gladius pattern short swords. As far as Thaddeus was concerned, the soldiers before him were amongst the best in all the world, their only equal being others of their kin. Upon seeing them, mustered as they were, he felt a swell of pride within his chest.

Magnificent. If only there were a ten score more legions like this, then surely it would be dwarf-kind that ruled the world.

In no time at all, the Centurion gave a nod to Thaddeus, all the legionaries were assembled, each standing at attention and ready for whatever was about to be asked of them. Pacing at the front of the assembled soldiers, absentmindedly inspecting their gear, Thaddeus bellowed.

'At ease!'

With a unified clank of metal grating on metal, the assembled legionaries moved their legs to a shoulder's width apart. Then a thud sounded as, again in perfect unison, each soldier rammed their shield into the parade ground's dirt, leaning them vertically against their legs.

'I have the misfortune of informing you all today that our great empire has suffered a major transgression at the hands of the human scum. They would like nothing more than to see our people destroyed. To claim everything that we have built as their own. To remove our legacy from the annuls of history. But we will not go quietly! In the face of certain doom, a plan has been formulated. A plan that will see our people endure and in time, gods willing, see us thrive once again. However, for it to succeed, a sacrifice will be required. So, I ask you this, who here is willing to die for our people!'

In response, every single dwarf upon that field, thrust their sword-arms into the air, whilst shouting at the top of their lungs, huh, huh, huh.

'I expected nothing less from the Empire's finest, you each do your ancestors proud. I would happily march, fight, and die alongside any of you. But, alas, this cannot be. Please know that I raise no questions as to your bravery, I know each of you has that in spades, no, this is a question of practicality. On the morrow our city will empty, bound for the capital. The citizenry, soft and unused to the hardships of the wild, will need guards for the journey. They will need you. So, to serve as our people's protectors, I ask those who have children yet unable to walk to remove yourselves from the parade grounds.'

Without a question, or complaint, a large cohort of legionaries picked up their shields, took a single step forward, before wheeling to their right and marching from the grounds.

'Next, those who's partners are expecting a child, remove yourselves.'

More dwarves silently left in an identical manner to those who had departed before them.

'Finally, those who are their parents only child or the last of their line, remove yourselves.'

Yet more dwarves left the grounds. Of those who remained, numbering no more than three hundred, Thaddeus looked deep into each of their eyes and bowed his head in respect.

'To those who are left, when the rest of the city departs for the capital tomorrow, we will not be with them. Instead, our mission is to ride to the Septentrionalem Pass. Once there, we will wait for the humans and stop them from traversing the pass for as long as we can. The longer we hold, the less time they will have to assault our people, the more of our kin will make it to safety. This is a delaying strategy nothing more, but an essential one.'

Thaddeus inhaled deeply, the legionaries made not a sound and moved not an inch.

'I have no doubt that we will exact a heavy toll upon them. They will learn to fear the legion once more, for this is a lesson that we will teach them. Now, go, sleep well, and prepare, for tomorrow we leave, perhaps to never return. Dismissed!'

As if they acted with one mind, the legionaries stood to attention and slapped their chests with closed fists. Thaddeus said nothing, but nodded his head to the dwarves. Instantly, they broke ranks and went back to their business, no doubt ruminating on the days to come.

Only once everyone else had left, Thaddeus departed the parade ground with a sense of foreboding building in his chest. He tried to ignore it as he got a bowl of stew from the mess, but as he ate, the feeling only intensified.

I sense my death approaching, that is all. Nothing to worry about.

Once his meal was finished, Thaddeus found an unoccupied cot in the barracks, collapsed onto it, and immediately passed out.

*   *   *

When Thaddeus awoke it was dark. A cacophony of snores, grunts, and mid-dream murmurs surrounded him as the city's legionaries slumbered.

Good. I'm glad that I woke up so early. Or is it still late? No matter.

After he emptied his bladder into an already half-full chamber pot, he left the barracks. Departing the fort, he walked along the cobbled road, climbing higher up the hill upon which the city sat. He rarely ventured into this part of the town as he found no joy in the intricate architecture of the well-to-do dwarf, for he had simple tastes.

Then, there was the fact that he found those of society's upper echelons to be both snobbish and vulgar. If it were not for Karissa, he would never enter this part of the city at all.

Walking by the fancy houses, with their well-trimmed pot plants and entirely unnecessary marble statues, he paid them no heed. They were not why he was here and meant nothing to him. Only one dwelling held any significance to him, and even then, it was not for the structure itself, but for the memories of what he had done within its walls, and with whom he had done them with.

Karissa, my love. What poor tidings do I bring thee.

When he reached his destination, he stopped and studied the house before him intently. The mansion, for that is what it was, stood three stories high and was at least five times as wide as what it was tall. It was large, but not uncommonly so, and no less ostentatious than those around it. Painted in a dark shade of blue, it stood out amongst the softer colours of its neighbours. Strangely, smoke still trailed lazily from two of its six chimneys.

Odd. I would have thought everyone would have retired by now. It seems that my good fortune continues.

Walking to the front door of the house, Thaddcus knocked. After a brief wait, the door was opened by a balding dwarf, clearly in his twilight years, who issued Thaddeus with a both greeting and a question.

'Good evening, sir. How can I be of service?'

'Good evening indeed. I need to have words with Karissa. I would appreciate it to the uttermost if you would be so kind as to fetch her, please.'

With a stony face, that hid all emotions that the butler may or may not have had, the elderly dwarf sighed before continuing to speak in a monotone drawl.

'My apologies sir. The mistress is asleep and has instructed me not to wake her. Perhaps sir could return in the morning? I'm sure that she'll be available to entertain guests then.'

Although he tried to contain it, frustration, coupled with a hint of anger, was etched clear on Thaddeus's tongue as he responded.

'I'm afraid, my good dwarf, that I will be unable to return tomorrow, or any day thereafter. I am Karissa's betrothed and I need to see her immediately. Fetch her this instant.'

At first, the butler looked as though he was going to refuse, raising nothing more than an eyebrow at the indignation of Thaddeus's demand. However, the slightest of glances into Thaddeus's eyes, and the detection of the murderous intent that boiled within them, dissuaded any such notion.

'As sir wishes.'

Bowing, before he closed the door, the butler left. Thaddeus waited.

One, two, and then five more minutes passed. Thaddeus was growing impatient and on the verge of storming into the house, propriety be damned, when the door re-opened and a vision of true angelic beauty leapt into his arms.

With a figure that every male dwarf longed for, and every female dwarf desired to possess, Karissa's dress clung tight against her long legs and perfectly thin waist. Low cut, it displayed more of her ample bosom than what would have been considered appropriate, but Thaddeus was grateful for the display.

If her father saw her now, he would not be happy.

Flawless skin of perfect porcelain surrounded a pair of rosebud soft lips. Hazel eyes, large, round, and ever inquisitive, sat as perfect mirrors to a soul of boundless mirth and kindness. Atop her head lay a crown of silken fire. Long and ever flowing, it fell to the small of her back, wafting gently as she moved, as if there were a breeze most quiet.

'Thaddeus, my love, it is you! Gods be praised. I could barely believe Geoffroy when he told me that you were here.'

Parting her hair lovingly, Thaddeus kissed Karissa tenderly on her forehead.

'I also praise the gods that I am here, but alas my heart is filled with sorrow for I am certain that our time together will be painfully short. Come, I have much to discuss with you and I would enjoy the night air and sweet scents of the orchard in your company one last time.'

Karissa's confusion gave way to worry after but a moment's pause.

'Dear Thaddeus, whatever do you mean?

'Don't fret my love, I'll explain everything as we go.'

'But what of father, what should I tell him? You know how he feels about our union and a traipse together unchaperoned; I do believe he'd have a coronary.'

'Well then, perhaps we'd best not tell him about it. Let him sleep and let us be away.'

Karissa giggled, her laughter sounding as a nightingale's cry.

'Oh my, how naughty. Alrighty then, my love, lead on.'

Stars twinkled in the sky above as the moons guided their path. Hand in hand, Thaddeus led Karissa through the orchard, the sweet aroma of apple blossoms a balm for his senses. Along the way, he told her of everything that had happened to him since their last meeting, deliberately omitting the nastier aspects of soldiering. She also told him of all her news, no matter how trivial. For a time, they were happy, content to just be together.

Alas, all mirth ended when Thaddeus told Karissa of his upcoming mission. As they reached their favourite spot, at the foot of the largest tree in the grove, Thaddeus embraced his betrothed, caressing her silken hair as he stared lovingly into her eyes.

'I would rather nothing than to stay forever in your arms. To sire an entire brood of children with you. To spend the rest of my life growing old alongside you, content that I have lived the best life any dwarf could ever hope to have lived. But I'm afraid that this is nothing more than a dream that I will never realise. I love you more than anyone has ever loved another, but I must go. For if I don't our people will suffer, more than they have any right to, but, more importantly to me, you will suffer. That I cannot abide.'

Tears welled in Karissa's eyes, the sight of which pained Thaddeus's heart to the verge of breaking.

'And what of me Thaddeus? What of me? How will I cope when I know that you'll never return to my side? How do you expect me to deal with the saddening truth that I'll never again know your touch, never taste your lips, never see your smile, or hear your laugh? I love you more than anything Thaddeus, and I would prefer death to being parted from your side. Please, don't leave me.'

Thaddeus could barely contain his emotions. Tears flowed from his eyes, scoring tracks through the dirt and grime upon his cheeks.

'I know that my love, by the gods don't I know that. If I forwent every shred of honour I have, I would take you with me and flee this instant. I would find us a ship to carry us far away from this forsaken land and we would be free to revel in our endless love for each other. But answer me this. What kind of a dwarf would I be to you then?'

Karissa sniffled back a sob.

'As long as I had you, I wouldn't care.'

'Bah, I'd be honourless and wretched. No longer able to face you with pride. I would become something lesser, something to be pitied. I would no longer be deserving of your love, and although I know you'll deny it now, eventually you'd grow to resent me. The love that we would have fought so hard to preserve would wither and die despite our efforts. Regardless of our desires, I must go.'

Karissa sighed as she accepted defeat, her own face glimmering as she wept openly.

'If you must go, I would have you. I would have you now.'

For a moment, Thaddeus was taken aback when Karissa grasped the back of his neck and pulled him close. Planting her lips on his, Karissa kissed Thaddeus with a passion and intensity he had never experienced before. Her tongue darted into his mouth, sending sparks through his body as it contacted his own. Impassioned, Thaddeus reciprocated, flicking his tongue into Karissa's mouth.

However, passion soon gave way to reason and Thaddeus broke away from Karissa, concern etched deep in his face.

'What of your prospects my love? None of good standing will marry a blemished woman, irrespective of her beauty or wealth. We

61

could stop this now before it went too far. You could still find love with another and lead a normal life without me.'

Angry at being stopped, Karissa scowled at Thaddeus.

'Do you think that I don't know that? If we lay together this night, I know full well what my future will hold. But hear me, Thaddeus, when I say that I do not care. I have chosen you. For now, and for always, I will only love you. For me, there is no one else and there never will be.'

'But, how can you know that? You are still young, with centuries yet to live. In the future a lord, or maybe even a prince, may catch your eye and…'

Karissa stopped Thaddeus mid-sentence by placing her finger over his lips.

'Hush, I want you, for I pray that from our union a child will grow within me. Then, no matter what happens, I will always have a part of you close to me. Forever. Now, shut up and fuck me.'

No longer able to deny his urges, Thaddeus grasped Karissa's buttocks with his hands. As he squeezed and caressed them, Karrisa, with her hands still around his neck, plunged her mouth onto his once more. Heat coursed through his entire body, his face flushed and his loins stirred in arousal.

Karissa hiked up the hem of her dress and with tender care Thaddeus started to rub her womanhood. To match his own, Karissa's face turned red as she moaned. Returning the favour, she unbuttoned Thaddeus's britches and pulled them down to his ankles. Fully erect, his manhood stood ready, throbbing in pace with his racing heartbeat. Despite himself, he groaned in appreciation as Karissa stroked his member, causing his head to swim with pleasure.

Wanting her more than he had ever wanted her before, Thaddeus grasped Karissa's thighs and lifted her from her feet. Pinning her to the trunk of the apple tree behind her, he spread her legs open. As the tip of his cock hovered dangerously close to her vagina, he could feel the waves of heat that emanated from her womanhood. Clutching his member tightly in her hands, Karissa nodded to Thaddeus.

With Karissa acting as his guide, Thaddeus slowly eased his stiff cock into Karissa. Her maidenhead presented but the briefest of resistances as he thrust himself through its wall. Karissa's nails bit deep into Thaddeus's shoulders as she released a pleasured scream. A damp warmth embraced Thaddeus's manhood and he knew what it was like to know true pleasure.

Pulling back, only to thrust himself deeper, Thaddeus was soon lost to the revelry of the flesh. It was beyond bliss, at every moment he felt himself upon the verge of collapse and expiration, yet he continued pumping himself in and out of Karissa, his grunts matched by her frenzied moans.

Soon, both were panting, unable to fuel their bodies with the oxygen they so desperately needed. Each were coated in a thick film of sweat, yet neither cared. Too soon for his liking, Thaddeus reached his limits. Unable to hold on any more, he gave one final thrust, as deep as he could, and exclaimed loudly as several thick spurts of seed shot from the tip of his member into Karissa's deepest parts.

For several moments, Thaddeus stayed where he was, simply staring lovingly into Karissa's eyes as he held her. Eventually, he withdrew himself from inside her and eased her gently to the ground. Pulling up his britches, he kissed her one last time. Taking her hand in his, he led her from the orchard. Along the way, neither said a single word, for each had already said everything that they had needed to say.

Once they reached the front of Karissa's house, they stopped, facing each other once more. Thaddeus kissed Karissa tenderly on her lips as he whispered to her.

'I love you.'

With a slew of fresh tears threatening to fall, Karissa mumbled back to him.

'I love you to.'

Not wanting to prolong their painful goodbyes, Karissa broke Thaddeus's embrace and walked inside. Simultaneously, Thaddeus turned towards the barracks and marched away. Neither of them looked back.

*   *   *

Overcame by a bevy of emotions, Thaddeus's racing brain prevented him from sleeping. As the hours dragged on, all he could think about was the touch of Karissa's lips and the warmth of her body against his. He longed for her, so much more than he had ever done so before, yet he knew that his desires had to be abandoned, if only for her sake. As rational as his logic behind their parting was, it still broke his heart.

Blessed relief from his incessant ruminations came as the mustering horn blew its morning call and he was summoned to action. Even though the sun had yet to rise, dwarves of every ilk climbed from their bunks, rubbing the persistent sleep from their eyes. Those that were destined to accompany the city's citizens to the capital, disseminated themselves throughout the city, rousing those who had not yet woken, assisting them in their preparations. The remaining legionaries, readied their rockclimbers, all the city had to offer, by loading them with as much provisions as they could comfortably carry.

Once assembled, Thaddeus's dwarves painted an impressive picture. Three hundred plate-clad legionaries atop three hundred naturally armoured steeds, lances in hand, ready to ride. Looking over his troops, Thaddeus felt nothing but pride. He knew that they were all going to die. He knew that he was going to die. He knew that he would never see Karissa again. But in that moment, the anticipation of battle rendered all his doubts moot.

Bringing his horn to his lips, Thaddeus gave it one long blast. The column of rockclimbers poured from the barracks, exiting the city's northern gate in an organised flood. For two days they rode, each day pushing their mounts to the verge of collapse. It was on the third day, just as the sun's rays were cresting the horizon, that at last they reached the pass. Thaddeus was pleased, for the humans had not yet made it that far south, but he was also anxious, for he knew that they would be close.

We've beaten the buggers here, but they must be close. We'd best prepare with all haste.

After dispatching a pair of scouts through the pass, to provide him with an early warning of his foes approach, Thaddeus set the remainder of the dwarves to task, building the basest of fortifications. To begin with they dug a trench. Going was slower than Thaddeus would have liked, as the earth was hardpacked, but as they were used to mining harder materials than dirt, they progressed steadily. Then, pushing the spoil to one side of the channel, they formed an earthen wall, atop of which they could stand. Now it was they, who would have the height advantage.

Seeing nothing more of note to do, and not wanting to tire his legionaries too much, Thaddeus ordered his men to stop. Then, they took to waiting. The first day passed without incident, the scouts did not return and there were no signs of humans. It was on the second day that the scouts returned, seeking out Thaddeus as soon as they had arrived back at camp.

'Commander! The human forces are close, they will be here presently.'

'So soon? How are they so close behind you?'

The scout grimaced as he responded.

'Their fucking outriders snuck up on us and we were caught unawares. They bogged us down with hit and run raids. We tried to escape, more than once, but they kept on cutting us off. In the end, we just barely managed it.'

'Gods be damned! No matter, what's done is done. What of their numbers and unit composition?'

The scout shook his head and then bowed in a request for forgiveness.

'Apologies commander. We only caught the barest of glimpses before we were engaged by their scouts. I don't know their exact numbers, but I know that there's a lot of them. Far more than any of our reports have indicated. As to their resources, I know nothing.'

'This is grim news indeed, but not completely unexpected. You and your fellows have done well to give us as much warning as you have. Rest now, as much as you can. I have a feeling we'll need you and your men on the line soon enough.'

Thaddeus raised his voice so all in the camp could hear him.

'Form up! Prepare for combat! The humans approach. Take to your stations!'

The camp buzzed with activity as each of the dwarves stopped what they were doing, which for the most part was either eating or sleeping,   and took their places upon the earthen rampart. Shielded and clad in the best steel their kind had to offer, they presented an impregnable wall that shimmered in the sunlight. Thaddeus took his place at the centre of the line, and with his kin he waited.

Time lost all semblance of meaning as the legionaries stood at ease. Thaddeus had no notion of how long it took for the human armies to reach the mouth of the pass, but reach it they did. First it was their flags and banners that crested the horizon, waving in the gentle breeze as the heralds of doom. Then came the men themselves, a wall of ragtag humans garbed in a motley collection of leathers and furs. They stopped their advance before they entered bow-range, the extent of their numbers still hidden behind the curve of the skyline.

With a white flag raised high, sitting atop a ragged horse, one of the humans approached the dwarven line. Thaddeus raised his hand, signalling to his troops that the man would be allowed parley. A half-dozen dwarves lowered their crossbows, yet another score kept theirs raised, ever wary of treachery. As he reached them, the man's steed skittered nervously along the edge of the trench, afeard of the pitfall. The man himself presented a fine figure, calm, collected, and confident. With a powerful, booming, voice he addressed the dwarven line.

'Who here is in command?'

Thaddeus remained stoically motionless as he responded to the rider, his voice louder than that of the man.

I'll not lose a shouting match to a human. Bloody scum.

'That would be me, human. Now, to be frank, I don't want to hear whatever it is you have to say, but I shall not dishonour the banner of truce, so say your piece and then bugger off!'

Steering his mount so that it came to a standstill in front of Thaddeus, the man continued, no longer shouting.

'I have been commanded by his esteemed majesty Lord Dalinar to beg of you and your people, for one final time, to sign the peace accord and end this war. We have no desire to slay you, or your kin, but your stubbornness in refusing to negotiate is rendering such an outcome nigh but inevitable. We are willing to allow you and the entirety of your kin safe passage from the proposed borders of our territory as a sign of good faith, but your people must leave Immediately. This is not negotiable.'

Thaddeus felt anger swell within his chest. This human deigned to dictate terms to him. This barbarian believed that he had a rightful claim over Thaddeus's homeland, where he was born and raised. Where countless generations of dwarf kind had lived, died, and prospered. This man just expected the entire dwarven race to pick up their lives and move because some arsehole by the name of Dalinar decreed it to be so. The arrogance of it all. Shaking with fury, Thaddeus responded in hushed tones, his rage etched deep upon his words.

'I will not move. For you. For your lord. Or for any of your kind. These lands are ours, if you want them, just try to take them.'

The rider spun his horse in a circle. Agitated by the entire ordeal, it pawed at the ground as the man shouted his response.

'So be it! Let the deaths that are to come rest heavily upon your conscience!'

Whipping his reigns and spurring the flank of his steed, the man thundered from the dwarven line. Thaddeus turned to the legionary by his side.

'Aren't these bloody humans arrogant? I think it would be for the best if we cured them of that. What do you reckon?'

Amused by his humour, all of those within earshot chuckled.

'All right lads, listen up. Those of you in the first rank, hold fast and don't let them through. We're all counting on you. When they get close, throw your axes into their heads, but don't break the wall. No matter what.'

As one, every dwarf in the front row shouted, 'huh, huh, huh.'

'Those in the second rank, shoot the buggers as soon as they're in range. Don't waste time picking your targets, just fire as quick as you can.'

Just as those in the first row had done, the voice of every dwarf in the second rank bellowed out in unison, 'huh, huh, huh.'

'Those in the third, fill any gaps in the line that crop up and reload any spare crossbows for the second rank to fire. In addition, hold up your shields to give us some aerial cover. I don't want to get taken out by some human peasant's errant shot.'

Louder than the others, the third rank chanted, 'huh, huh, huh.'

'Now then lads, let's teach them to fear the legion! No quarter given, nor asked for! Kill the fuckers, before they kill you or your brothers!'

A thunderous cheer erupted from the dwarven line. In unison, they pounded the face of their shields, or, for those that held no shield, their chest-plate, with their steel-clad fists. Within his chest, Thaddeus felt the blood lust rise. It was a familiar feeling, one he encountered before every battle, yet he had never explained it to another before. However, standing alongside his brethren, the air electric with emotions, he knew that they all felt as he did. They all longed to kill.

Come on you human fuckers, come at me. My blade's thirsty for your blood. Argh!

Over the horizon, the humans echoed the dwarven cheer with one of their own, then charged. As they drew ever nearer, a wall of scuttling flesh, Thaddeus felt his heartrate surge as the anticipation grew. Gripping the hilt of his sword, more tightly than practical, he licked his lips as a cold sweat formed upon his brow.

Almost there, come on now.

Without a single word of command being issued, dwarven bowstrings thrummed a constant symphony of death as the humans entered their range. Men screamed and fell wounded, only to be crushed by their compatriots, or fell silent, already dead. Handfuls of human arrows pattered against the dwarven line, but found no purchase as they were ineffectual against the dwarves' sturdy armour and stout shields.

Reaching the trench, the human horde stopped their advance, unsure of what to do. As one, the dwarves of the first rank loosed their throwing axes in two rapid volleys. Countless men crumpled as their bodies were shattered, heavy dwarven steel lodged firmly in their chests and heads. Some of the humans threw their spears at the dwarves, but just like the arrows, they bounced harmlessly off of the dwarven shield wall.

Below him, the trench began to fill with human corpses.

At this rate the ditch will fill long before their horde is defeated. They'll be able to use the bodies of their kin as a bridge. Our advantage will be lost. No matter.

An unfamiliar horn blared over the din of battle. Instantly, the humans stopped their offensive and fell back, clambering over the dead and the dying in a frantic bid for safety. His kin continued to shoot the fleeing humans. Uneasy with slaughtering anyone in such a dishonourable manner, Thaddeus considered ordering a cessation of fire, but quickly disregarded the notion as foolish.

This is war. There is no honour in war. They die, or we do. That's all there is to it.

As the final man in range fell, his back peppered with a trio of crossbow bolts, the dwarven bows fell silent, their owners waiting for their foe to return.

Thaddeus scanned the battlefield before him, assessing both the humans' position and their losses. The ground was littered thick with their dead, slick with blood and other bodily fluids. Some, a scant few, law moaning as they died, succumbing to either blood loss or trauma. Most were already dead, silent, motionless. Not a single dwarf had fallen.

Afeard, or just needing to regroup, Thaddeus knew not, the humans disappeared over the horizon. The dwarf line cheered, elated by their resounding victory, yet Thaddeus remained silent. He knew that they would be back. It was just a matter of time.

This is only a small victory. Still a victory, but inconsequential to the whole.

Upon the dawn of the next day, the humans came again. As a roiling wave of shouting fury, they stampeded into the pass, seemingly irreverent to the rotting corpses of their deceased comrades. Just as they had the day before, their assault broke harmlessly upon the wall of dwarven steel that barred their way. Hundreds, if not thousands, died, yet not one was a dwarf.

One hour past noon on the third day, they returned, only to suffer the same fate as the two days previous. On the fourth day, the humans eschewed combat, instead they remained hidden beyond the horizon. For the dwarves this was a blessed relief, as it allowed them to restock their almost depleted stores of ammunition by collecting it from the dead.

It was on the morning of the fifth day, two hours before noon, when the humans returned. However, instead of charging the dwarves, they halted their advance just beyond crossbow range. And, much to Thaddeus's surprise, formed themselves into orderly ranks.

So much for being a horde of barbarian simpletons. Unlike the others, these buggers have clearly been trained. But by whom I wonder?

Finding the silence, but more so the standoff, unnerving, Thaddeus shifted uneasily on his feet. Mercifully, his waiting was short-lived as the human ranks parted. Riding through the newly formed passage was a singular figure, massive, and as far as Thaddeus could tell from that distance, not human.

Who in the bloody seven hells is that? Their leader? Gods that fucker's huge.

Sitting atop an armoured sabre lion, the man swayed as his mount stalked gracefully towards the dwarven line. In one hand he held a spear, in the other a shield. An ornately carved breastplate shone upon his chest and purple plumes fluttered from the top of his Corinthian helm.

Even from this distance, Thaddeus sensed an aura of danger emanating from the figure. His gut prompted him to riddle the man with bolts, to kill him before he could get close. However, before he could issue the order, he was stopped by the sight of a white flag that was draped from the haft of his spear.

Bah, fucking parley, truces are bullshit. True, it'll buy us some time, but I'd prefer to be fighting.

At a distance of some thirty feet, the rider stopped. It was at this point that Thaddeus noted that, in contrary to his early belief that the man was not human, the man was in fact so, albeit the largest one he had ever seen.

Around nine feet tall, I'd guess. I didn't know that they grew that big. Bugger me.

The man's head swivelled from side to side as he inspected the dwarven forces. Then, with no apparent effort, he shouted to the dwarves, his voice crystal clear to their entire line, irrespective of the distance.

'To say that I was disappointed when I heard that you had rejected my offer for clemency, would be quite the understatement. I fully expected to be much further south by now, oh well, no matter. Now, which of you is in charge?'

Silently, Thaddeus raised his hand.

'Capital. I Lord Dalinar, Supreme Commander of the United Tribes, hereby challenge you to single combat. Battle shall commence immediately, and will only end upon the death of one, or both, of the combatants. Failure to comply will result in the swift and utter destruction of you and your fellows.'

As he made this remark, Dalinar gestured to the human forces behind him. As if on cue, they parted to reveal a line of ballistae, each loaded and ready to fire. Thaddeus's heart sunk as he noticed that the tips of their bolts glowed with a flickering green light.

Fuck.

'I hear that death by eldritch fire is quite excruciating, something to be avoided, I'm sure. Now, to terms. Should you win our duel, the remainder of my army will disband and leave your people unmolested for the next ten years. That should give you plenty of time to ready yourselves for their next offensive.'

Bloody generous of him. Pillock.

'If I should win, your forces will stand down. They will be guaranteed safe passage past the border of our proposed territory, as will the remainder of your kin still north of this border. What say you?'

With a heavy heart, Thaddeus sighed. He had no choice and he knew it. There was no way his forces could withstand the bombardments of ballistae, let alone magically enhanced ballistae. He would have to accept Dalinar's duel, for at least then his soldiers would live.

I hate it, but it if it is fated to be, then so be it.

Walking down from the earthen mound, taking extra care with his footing, lest he fall and embarrass himself, Thaddeus leapt across the trench in a single leap before addressing the man.

'I accept your terms, Dalinar, but answer me this. Will you be fighting from atop your steed, whereas I will be on foot? Surely not, for there would be little honour in such an unfair contest.'

'Ha, ha. Of course not, dwarfling.'

Thaddeus examined Dalinar as he slid effortlessly from the back of his mount. He moved with a poise and a balance that alluded to a great level of skill. The effortless way he carried his weapons made them seem weightless. He was a man that was both dexterous and strong, not to mention twice his height. This was going to be a difficult fight for him to win, maybe even impossible.

Bah, if I die, then so be it. I shan't quit, and I won't surrender. I can't afford to.

Dalinar squared off some twenty feet in front of Thaddeus, lowering his spear towards the dwarf , while covering his body with his shield. Ice blue eyes glared from beneath his helm as he smirked at Thaddeus, his confidence absolute.

'Shall we begin?'

Not bothering to respond, Thaddeus raised his own shield, holding it against his chest, and charged at Dalinar, his sword-hand wrapped firmly around the hilt of his sheathed blade.

Dalinar stood immobile as Thaddeus rushed towards him, but as the dwarf entered his reach, he unleashed a blood curdling scream and thrust his spear at Thaddeus's chest. Unable to avoid the blow, Thaddeus felt his arm numb as the spear-tip slammed into his shield with a force that he could barely conceive. In an instant, Thaddeus's charge was stopped as he was propelled backwards by the impact. Landing arse first onto the ground, he reacted instinctively and rolled aside, barely dodging a second spear thrust.

Rolling a second time, Thaddeus regained his footing. Drawing his sword, he swung it at Dalinar's side. His blade clattered harmlessly against the man's shield. Trying to move around Dalinar's guard, Thaddeus took another swing, but this strike was blocked as deftly as the first.

Amused, Dalinar laughed at Thaddeus's efforts.

'Ha, ha, come on dwarfling. Surely you can do better than that. Move those stunted legs just a little bit faster. Ha, ha.'

Punctuating his words, Dalinar swept his spear across the ground where Thaddeus stood. The shaft of Dalinar's weapon smacked into Thaddeus's legs and he felt his knees buckle. Unbidden, he fell to the ground once more.

Shit, get off the bloody ground. I can't win this from my back.

Leaping over Thaddeus's prone form, Dalinar slammed the rim of his shield into Thaddeus's stomach. Struggling under the immense pressure, his plate armour bent and buckled. As the pulverised steel was pushed into his gut, Thaddeus gasped as all the air in his lungs was forcibly expelled.

Deciding to not push his advantage further, Dalinar backed away from Thaddeus, giving him room to stand. Thaddeus got to his feet gingerly, swaying and breathing hard.

'That's the spirt dwarfling. I don't want this to be over just quite yet, not when I'm having this much fun.'

Enraged at being toyed with, Thaddeus charged at Dalinar once more. Whether it was from skill, dumb luck, or overconfidence on

Dalinar's part, Thaddeus's first swing slipped under the human's guard. The tip of his blade sliced across Dalinar's exposed thigh, cutting it as easily as paper. A thin red line now marked the human's flesh, its only blemish. But as it slowly wept, Dalinar simply smiled, to him the wound was nothing more than a novelty.

'So, it begins now.'

Wild eyed, Dalinar bellowed a deep and guttural scream. Slamming the shaft of his spear against the ground, the weapon began to shimmer and shift in his hands. The spear tip lengthened as the shaft shortened and, in nothing more than a moment, the spear was gone, replaced by a greatsword. Dark and twisted, it reeked of malice and foreboding.

Well, that's a neat trick.

At the same time, Dalinar's shield altered its form. Moving from his offhand, it wriggled up his arm, reforming itself into an overlarge puldron atop his shoulder.

And, if I'm being honest, also a tad disturbing.

Faster than what should have been possible for such a large being, Dalinar swept his sword across the face of Thaddeus's shield. Humming as it flew, the blade sliced through the dwarven steel as if it was nothing more than air. Rent in two, Thaddeus dropped the now useless shield, letting it clatter to the ground.

Not good.

Sensing an opening, Thaddeus stabbed his blade towards Dalinar's flank, but the human reacted with the speed of lightning. Mid-stroke, Dalinar stepped aside and caught the dwarf's arm, holding his firmly in place. With a manic desperation, Thaddeus tried to break the man's hold, but to no avail. He was helpless.

Having both caught his prey, and no longer finding interest in his game, Dalinar threw Thaddeus straight up into the air. Tumbling in circles as he flew, and then fell, he lost all semblance of direction and amidst the blur of motion, Dalinar had effectively disappeared.

Argh, oh gods, where in the seven hells did he go? I cannot see him.

On Thaddeus's downwards descent, Dalinar thrust his blade into Thaddeus's chest, picking him clean out of the air. While he hung suspended, Thaddeus's eyes went wide as Dalinar's blade burst through his body, exploding from his back in a shower of blood and gore. His arms went limp as his body went into shock. In that instant, he knew that he was going to die and that it would be soon.

Karissa. Oh Karissa, how I love you so.

Dalinar kicked Thaddeus from his sword and he went sprawling across the ground yet again. When he came to a stop, he gave everything that he had left to rise from the dirt. After a herculean effort, he knelt upon the earth, lungs heaving, blood oozing from the corners of his mouth, utterly spent. Even though he knew it to be futile, he pressed his hand firmly against the wound in his chest, trying in vain to stem the bleeding. His sword lay in the mud far outside of his reach, his shield, long since sundered, was just as useless. He had nothing, and there was nothing he could do.

With a casual gait, Dalinar walked over to him. He knew he had won the fight, just as Thaddeus knew that he had lost.

'You have fought surprisingly well dwarf. Tell me, what is your name?'

Thaddeus spat a thick globule of blood onto the ground beside him. Although it took all the strength he had left, he raised his head, staring daggers at Dalinar. As his blood dribbled down his chin, he gurgled in response.

'My name is Thaddeus.'

'Well Thaddeus, you are a testament to the tenacity of your kind. You will be long remembered. I will see to that.'

Dalinar's wrists tightened around the hilt of his great sword. Exhaling slowly, he lowered his blade to his side and gave a nod of respect to Thaddeus. Then, with one forward step, he swung the mighty sword alongside his body. Singing as it sliced through the air, the magical steel barely slowed as it passed through Thaddeus's neck. As his head was parted from his body, geysers of blood spurted from the dwarf's neck. Already dead, his limp corpse crumpled into the dirt as his head rolled to a stop in the ever-growing pool of crimson.

About the Author

M. J. Coad was born in 1989 in a small Australian town called Seymour, which is a smidge over 100km north of Melbourne. However, during his childhood, as an army brat, he moved frequently and has never considered Seymour to be his home. From an early age, he enjoyed reading and grew up on the fantastical tales of Tolkien, Rowling, Feist, Pratchett, and Martin. To name but a few. Throughout his six years of study at the University of Tasmania, culminating in a Masters of Teaching, he never really knew what he wanted to be, just that it was not a teacher. It was by chance, that he discovered the Critical Role YouTube channel and the world of tabletop RPG's. The spark of inspiration struck. Deciding to combine his love for reading with the joy he found in playing games, and watching others play them, he began to write, crafting a world of his own.

You can find out more about M. J. Coad, and his other works, on his website, mjcoad.com.au, where you can also join his mailing list. Ensure that you never miss out on a future book launch.

M. J. Coad's Other Works

Heroes of Thered's Field: Shadows of Ulandir Book One

All journeys have a beginning. All heroes have an origin. No one can succeed alone.

On the southern edges of continental Ulandir an ancient evil roils against its bonds. Shadows creep where the light once held sway and creatures, both freshly felled and long since dead, now walk once more in thrall. Yet, this is only the preamble to Térrtha's end times. There is still a chance that catastrophe can be avoided, slim though it be.

Touched by fate, and united through circumstance, a quintet of disparate individuals find themselves at the heart of this nightmare. Although each of these five are skilled in their own way, questions remain. Can they become more than what they are now? Will they surpass their limitations and overcome their demons? How can mere mortals defeat something that even the gods fear?

Heroes of Thered's Field is the first book in an epic dark fantasy series replete with action and abounding with grit.

Buy it now, in either a physical or an e-book format, from the author's website: mjcoad.com.au

www.ingramcontent.com/pod-product-compliance
Lightning Source LLC
Chambersburg PA
CBHW020546130626
46552CB00007B/2773